A NOTE TO PARENTS

When your children are ready to "step into reading," giving them the right books is as crucial as giving them the right food to eat. **Step into Reading Books** present exciting stories and information reinforced with lively, colorful illustrations that make learning to read fun, satisfying, and worthwhile. They are priced so that acquiring an entire library of them is affordable. And they are beginning readers with a difference—they're written on five levels.

Early Step into Reading Books are designed for brand-new readers, with large type and only one or two lines of very simple text per page. **Step 1 Books** feature the same easy-to-read type as the Early Step into Reading Books, but with more words per page. **Step 2 Books** are both longer and slightly more difficult, while **Step 3 Books** introduce readers to paragraphs and fully developed plot lines. **Step 4 Books** offer exciting nonfiction for the increasingly independent reader.

 Published in the United States by Random House, Inc., New York, and simultaneously in Canada by Random House of Canada Limited, Toronto.

http://www.randomhouse.com/

Library of Congress Cataloging-in-Publication Data:
Berenstain, Stan, 1923–
The Berenstain bears ride the thunderbolt / by Stan & Jan Berenstain.
p. cm. — (Step into reading) (An early step-into-reading book)
summary: The Bear family goes on a roller coaster ride.
ISBN 0-679-88718-0 (trade). — ISBN 0-679-98718-5 (lib. bdg.)
[1. Roller coasters—Fiction. 2. Bears—Fiction.]
I. Berenstain, Jan, 1923– . II. Title. III. Series. IV. Series: Early step-into-reading.
PZ7.B4483Bff 1998
[E]—dc21
97-36292

Printed in the United States of America 10 9 8 7 6 5 4 3 2 1

Stan & Jan Berenstain

Random House New York

The Thunderbolt!

THUNDERBOLT

Waiting in line.

Buying tickets.

Getting on.

Buckling up.

Going up.
Up, up, up!
Clickety-clickety
clackety-click!

At the top.

FUN

Going down.
Down, down, down!
Clackety-clackety
clickety-clack!

Down and around!

Upside down!

Into the dark!

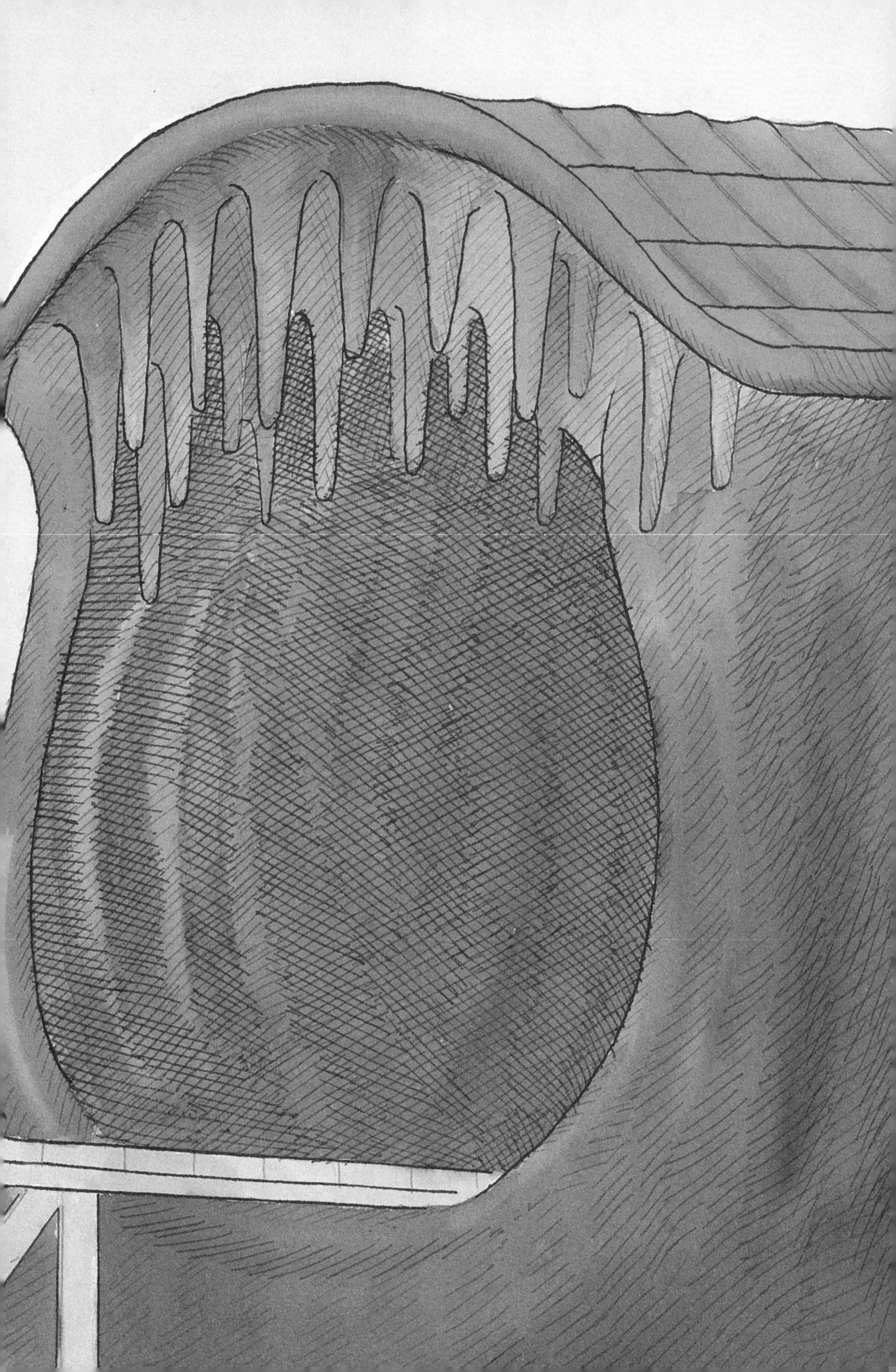

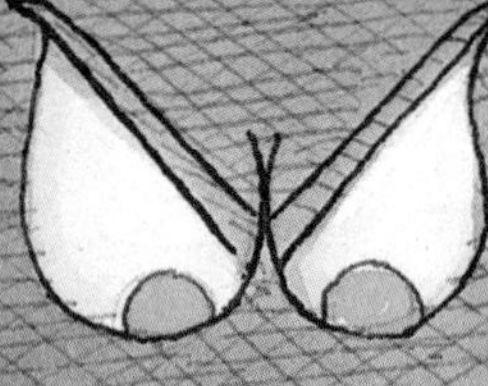

Look out!

Spooks!

Into the light.

Slowing down.

Getting off.

"Again! Again!
Do it again!"

"Not so quick!
Not so quick!
Your papa looks
a little sick."

"But that was fun!
That was fun!"

Going on again,
minus one.